AS THE NEWEST MEMBER OF AN INTERGALACTIC PEACEKEEPING
FORCE KNOWN AS THE GREEN LANTERN CORPS, HAL JORDAN
FIGHTS EVIL AND PROUDLY WEARS THE UNIFORM AND RING OF . . .

SUPER DC HEROES

GREEN LANTERN

WEB OF DOOM

WRITTEN BY
MICHAEL ANTHONY
STEELE

ILLUSTRATED BY
DAN SCHOENING

STONE ARCH BOOKS
a capstone imprint

Published by Stone Arch Books in 2012
A Capstone Imprint
151 Good Counsel Drive, P.O. Box 669
Mankato, Minnesota 56002
www.capstonepub.com

Library of Congress Cataloging-in-Publication Data
Steele, Michael Anthony.
  Web of doom / written by Michael Steele ; illustrated by Dan Schoening.
  p. cm. -- (DC super heroes)
  ISBN-13: 978-1-4342-2621-1 (library binding)
  ISBN-13: 978-1-4342-3407-0 (pbk.)
  1. Green Lantern (Fictitious character)--Juvenile fiction. 2. Superheroes--
Juvenile fiction. 3. Supervillains--Juvenile fiction. [1. Superheroes--Fiction. 2.
Supervillains--Fiction. 3. Science fiction.] I. Schoening, Dan, ill. II. Title.
  PZ7.S8147We 2012
  813--dc22   2011005155

Summary: HAL JORDAN can't get a break! He tries to free a fleet of
intergalactic battle cruisers from the energy webs of the ruthless KIRIAZIS.
But the crusiers don't want his help. The war-like race wants to fight their own
battles. Then, as KIRIAZIS spins her evil plans, another villain arrives and
causes problems for everyone. The only way out of this sticky situation is for
GREEN LANTERN to team up with his former foe. Can the two warriors
work together or will this epic battle become an epic failure?

Art Director: Bob Lentz and Brann Garvey
Designer: Hilary Wacholz
Production Specialist: Michelle Biedscheid

Printed in the United States of America in Stevens Point, Wisconsin.
032011
006111WZF11

TABLE OF CONTENTS

CHAPTER 1

CAUGHT IN THE CROSSFIRE

Hal Jordan was a Green Lantern. As a member of the Green Lantern Corps, Hal often took part in epic space battles. He performed daring rescues and saved entire planets from destruction. He wielded a power ring that gave him amazing abilities. It allowed him to travel the stars and visit many remarkable worlds and strange societies.

At this moment, however, Hal Jordan was extremely bored. He sat at the center of a long table with two others.

Hal had been assigned the task of overseeing the signing of a peace treaty between the planet Juray and the planet Talesca.

BANG! The Juray delegate slammed his meaty fist against the table. "Again, this is unacceptable!" he boomed. He tossed down the rewritten treaty. "Your shipping lanes trespass into Juray space."

The Talesca delegate turned up his nose. "Those lanes are for supply shipments for our outer colonies," he said, pointing a bony finger across the table. "You would have our colonists starve, then?"

Hal shook his head and stood. "All right," he said. He knew what he was about to say would be pointless. "I still think sharing those shipping lanes would be the best —"

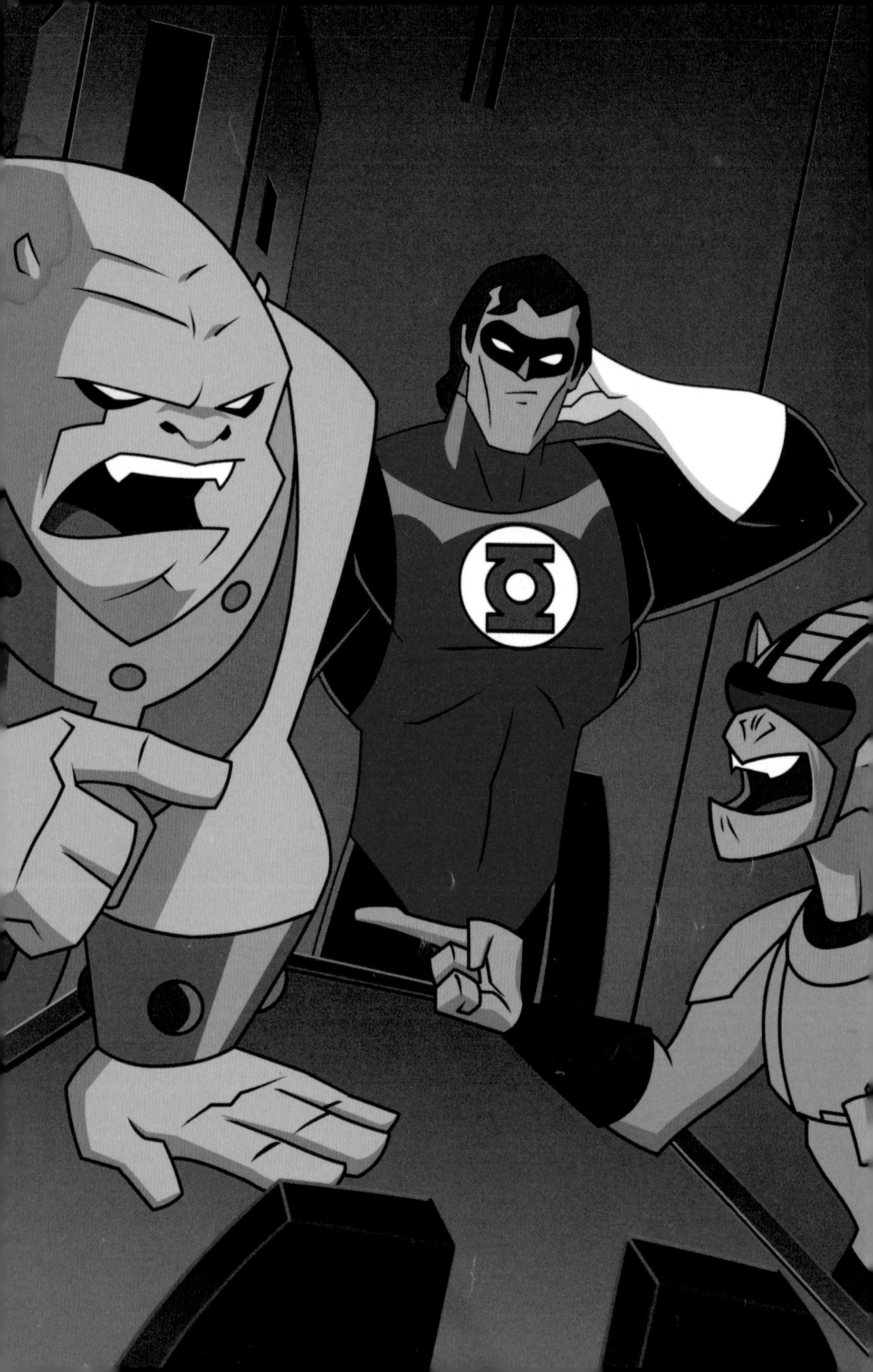

"Nonsense!" the Talesca delegate interrupted. "We've already rejected that idea."

The Juray delegate chuckled. "Yes, the Talescians clearly don't share," he said.

Hal sat back in his chair and yearned for a different assignment. He thought a planet-wide invasion would be easier to handle than these two.

At that moment, the chamber door opened, and the Juran's young aide entered. She walked to the Juray delegate and whispered something into his ear.

"What?!" he barked. Then he glared at the Talesca delegate. "How dare you!"

"How dare I what?" asked the Talescian.

The Juran swept his papers into his open satchel.

"These negotiations are over!" he shouted.

The Talescian snorted. "Typical."

Hal shot to his feet. "Wait a minute. What's the problem?" asked the hero.

The Juray delegate pointed a thick finger across the table. "These Talescian traitors have launched an attack!" he said.

The Talesca delegate jumped to his feet. "I resent that allegation! We agreed to these negotiations on good faith! We even requested the help of the Green Lantern Corps!" He was interrupted as one of his own aides entered the chamber and whispered into his ear.

Hal moved to the large Juray delegate. "What are you talking about?" he asked. "How were you attacked?"

The Juran finished packing his bag. "We've lost contact with our entire space fleet," he replied. "They were patrolling the asteroid belt between our two worlds, and now they're gone."

"Lies!" barked the Talesca delegate. "I've just been informed that our fleet is the one that has gone missing." He shook his fist. "This means war!"

As the two delegates stormed toward the exit, Hal raised his right fist. **ZZZAPPPPPPP!** A burst of green energy erupted from his power ring. The beam zigzagged past the delegates and formed a large brick wall in front of them. Their exit was blocked.

"What is the meaning of this?" asked the Juran.

"Just whose side are you on?" asked the Talescian.

"I'm not on anyone's side," Hal replied. "I just don't think you should do anything rash until we figure this out."

"There is nothing to figure out," boomed the Juran. "Those Talescian savages have attacked."

The Talesca delegate glared at the Juran. "Savages?! Why you —!"

Hal created a second brick wall, separating the delegates. "Let's just go see for ourselves, shall we?" the hero said.

*   *   *

After several hours, Hal Jordan finally convinced the delegates to investigate the missing space fleets. He rode with them as they took a space ship to the asteroid belt.

Hal could have flown there much faster using his ring, but he thought it best to stay close to the squabbling delegates.

The ship slowed as they approached the asteroid belt. The wide band of floating rocks acted as a natural border between the two planets. Both the Juray and Talesca space fleets patrolled their sides of the belt.

Earlier, Hal had seen the ships facing off on his way to the negotiations. Now, as Hal looked through the ship's viewport, the large battleships were nowhere to be seen.

"There, you see?" said the Juran delegate. "Our ships are gone!"

"No doubt they fled after they destroyed our fleet," said the Talescian.

"Now, listen," said Hal. "It's obvious that both fleets are gone."

Hal pointed to the asteroids. "Something odd is going on here," he began. "Let me investigate —"

The ship shook beneath Hal's feet. Several bright yellow bands crisscrossed the viewport. Hal peered out a side window and saw more yellow beams. Suddenly, the ship jolted as it was dragged forward. Asteroids zipped by as the ship was pulled toward an unknown destination.

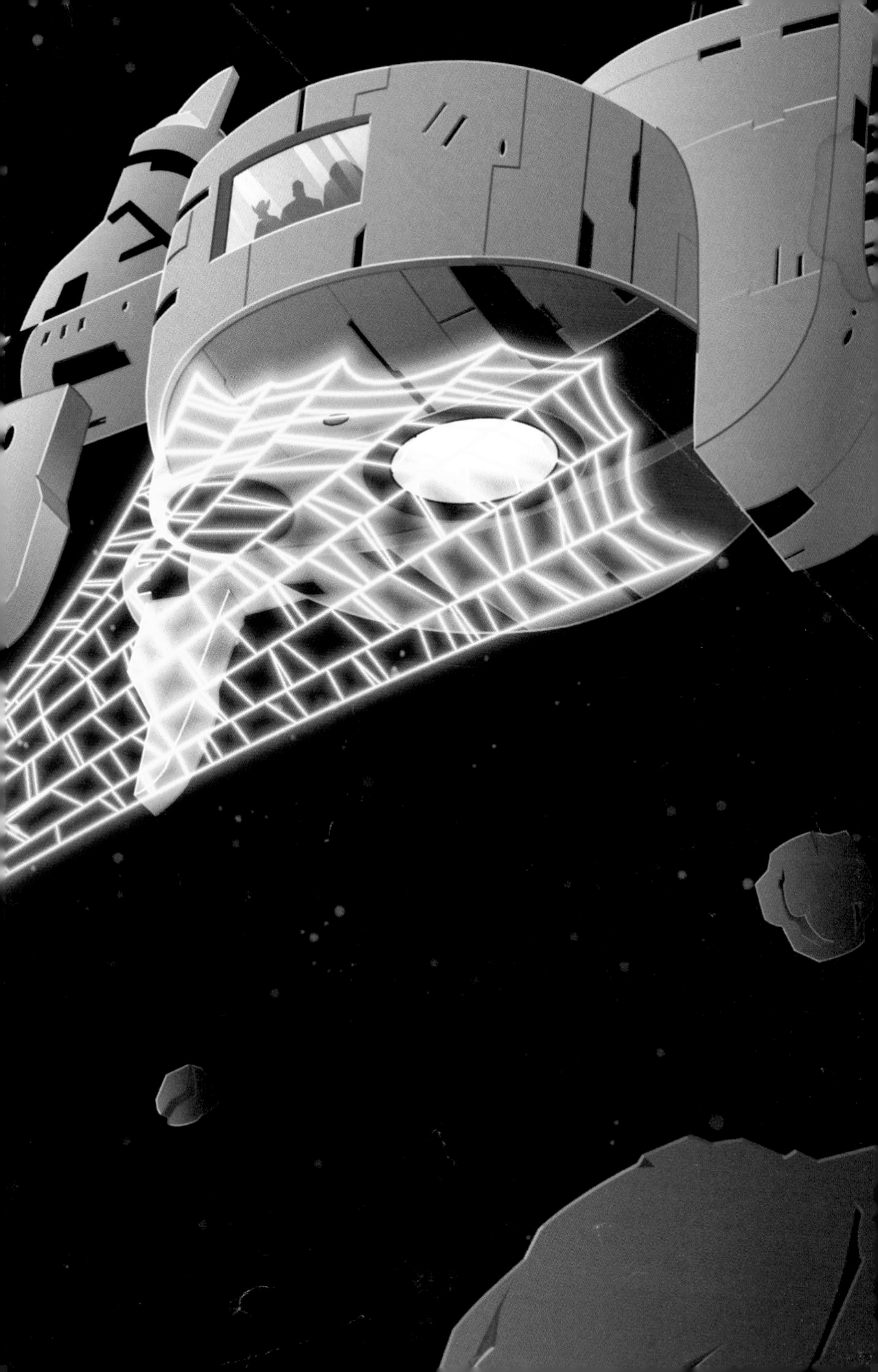

CHAPTER 2

TANGLED IN THE WEB

Giant balls of rock hurtled past the viewport as the ship snaked deeper into the asteroid belt. Soon, hundreds of ships came into view. They were packed tightly like a school of fish, trapped inside a net made of yellow energy beams. Beside them, an equal amount of ships were crowded inside another net. They were the two missing space fleets.

"What have you done?" asked the Juran.

"Us?! What have *you* —" began the Talescian.

Hal quickly cut them off. "All right, let's not start arguing again," he said. "It's clear to me that you have a common enemy."

"Preposterous," snorted the Talescian. The Juran merely shook his head.

Hal stepped closer to the two delegates. "Look, I'm going to step outside and investigate," he said. "You two try to get along for a while."

Hal walked to the air lock in the back of the ship. After sealing off the rest of the cabin, he opened the hatch and flew out into space. His ring created a thin force field that allowed him to breathe. Otherwise, he would have suffocated in the harsh emptiness of space.

Hal was barely able to squeeze through the yellow beams surrounding the ship.

Hal flew toward the nearest netted fleet. He had to figure out why they were trapped.

ZZRRRRTT! ZZRRRRTT!

The ships began firing their weapons at him. Laser beams erupted from barrels of large guns. Hal didn't have to worry about dodging the beams. They were absorbed by the yellow webbing holding the ships.

Hal raised his ring and opened a communication channel to the fleet. "Hold your fire!" he ordered. "I'm trying to help you."

"This is the Juran fleet admiral," boomed a voice from his ring. "Are the Green Lanterns siding with the Talescians? Is that why you've trapped us here, you traitors?!"

"Only the Jurans would be so treacherous," shouted another voice through his ring. It came from the other bundled fleet.

ZZRRRRRTT! The other fleet began firing their weapons. Just like the Juran fleet, the Talescian beams didn't get past the yellow netting.

Hal hovered between the two fleets. He originally planned on releasing the trapped ships. But if he did that now, they would blow each other apart.

Hal used his ring to speak. "Listen," he said. "Hold your fire for a minute while I figure out who did this to you."

At first, Hal didn't think the fleets would cooperate. Then, slowly, both sides stopped firing their weapons.

Finally, a little progress, Hal thought.

Hal flew closer to the Juran fleet and held up his ring. "Ring, analyze these energy webs," the hero commanded.

His ring never had a chance. *BAM!* Hal was hit hard from behind. He went tumbling through space. He increased the power of his force field just before slamming into an asteroid. *CRUNCH!* The rock crumbled into floating rubble.

Hal turned to see a fearsome alien woman flying toward him. She had spiked pink skin and four glowing eyes. She had sharp claws on each hand and small spikes covered her arms and legs.

What worried Hal was her uniform. She was a member of an evil group of aliens called the Yellow Lanterns.

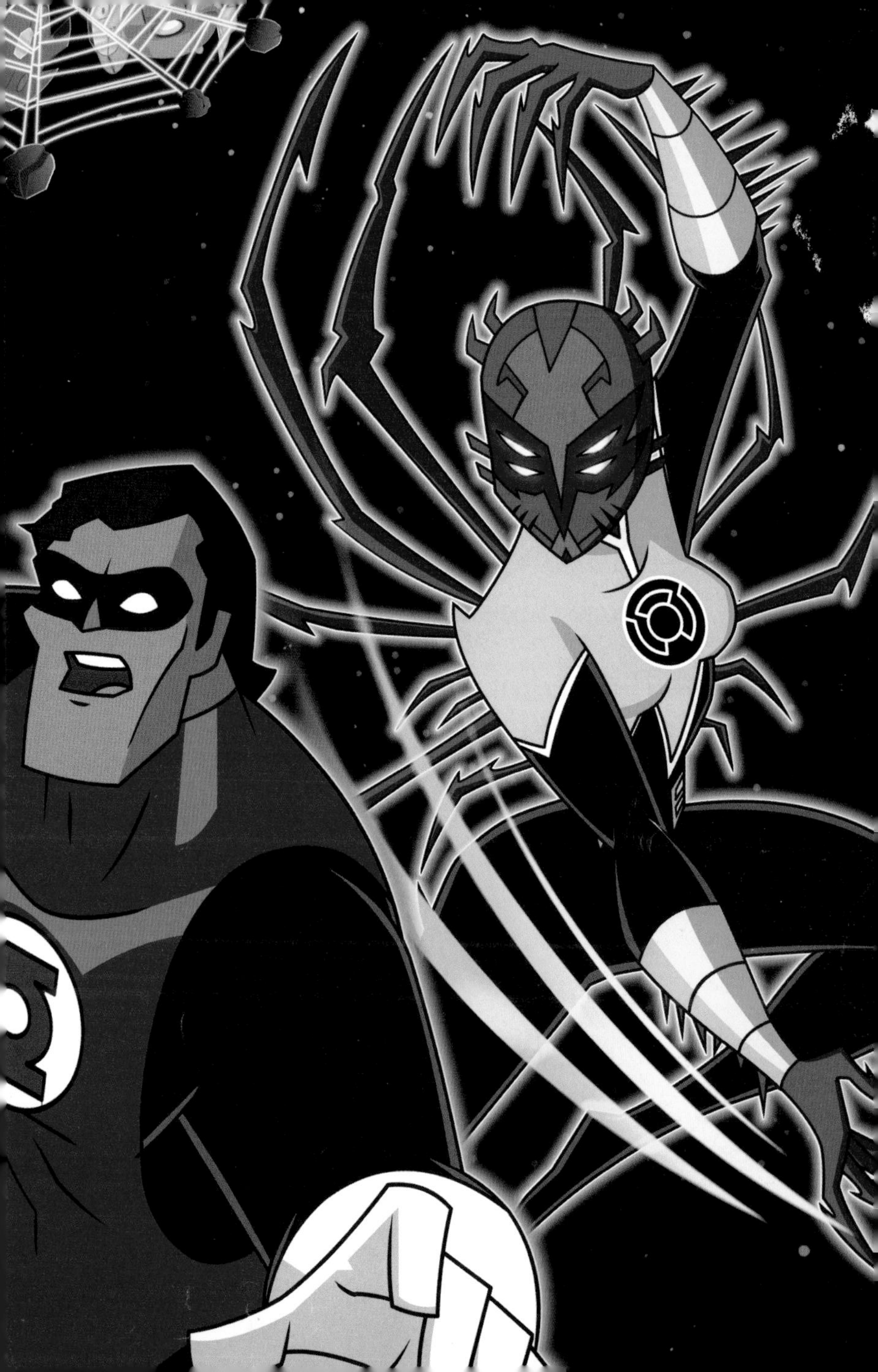

"Green Lantern," she growled. "You have no business here." She aimed her own power ring and a yellow beam of energy erupted from it.

Hal had his own ring create a green shield. He jolted as the beam bounced off. "I beg to differ," he said. "I'm Hal Jordan, Green Lantern of this sector — and I order you to release these ships!"

"Ah, Hal Jordan," she said as she slowly circled him. "You're quite famous. My name is Kiriazis, and I'm not so well-known." Her energy ring glowed. "That is, until I destroy you!" CRACKLE! CRACKLE!

She sent two yellow beams of energy zipping toward him. Hal easily dodged the first beam and deflected the second with his shield. However, the impact sent him flying backward.

Hal stopped when he hit something springy. He looked back to see a giant, yellow spider web stretched between several asteroids. That was why the first beam was so easy to dodge — it had created the web behind him!

Hal struggled to break free, but the yellow beams were sticky and very strong. Hal was trapped like a fly in a spider web.

Kiriazis flew closer and landed on one of the asteroids. Just like a spider, she nimbly crawled out onto the web. "All too easy," she hissed.

Hal struggled hard but still couldn't free himself. He had been sent to help create peace between Talesca and Juray. Now he would be destroyed as the two warring fleets watched helplessly.

Hal did not know that someone else was watching, too. A small orange figure named Glomulus peeked out from behind a nearby asteroid. The three-legged, four-armed, egg-shaped creature giggled with excitement. His master would be quite pleased by what he had found.

Glomulus pushed away from the asteroid and zipped off into space. Greedy for his master's approval, he flew as fast as he could.

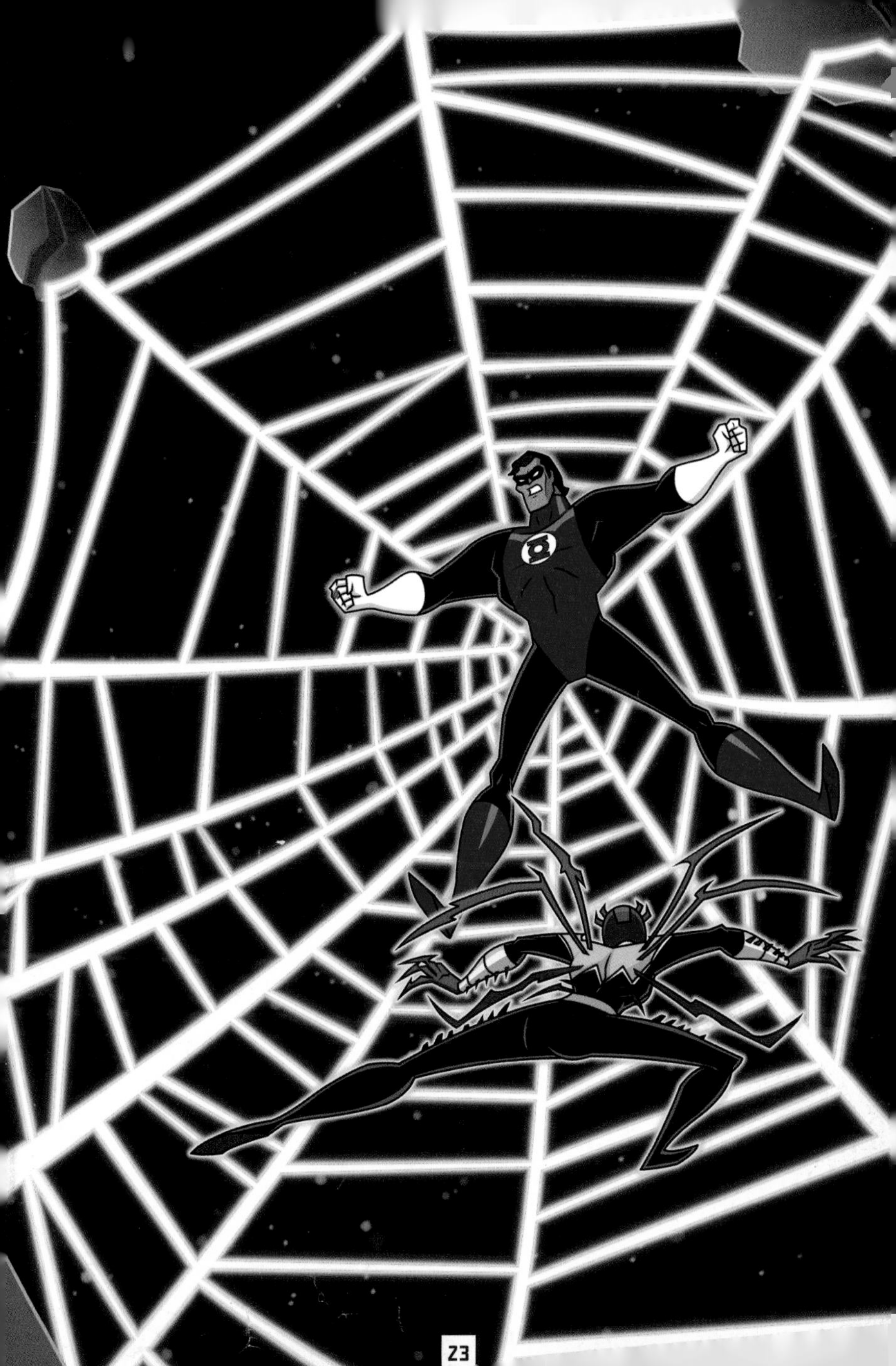

CHAPTER 3

ENTER LARFLEEZE

Hal smirked as Kiriazis crept closer.

"I get it," Hal said. "We're the flies, and you're the spider." His ring began to glow. "But guess what goes after spiders?"

PHWOOT! Hal created a giant green crow! The huge bird flapped its wings as it hovered over Kiriazis. It pecked at her with its sharp beak.

"Foul creature!" Kiriazis shouted. She sprung off the web. As the giant bird flew closer, it chased her away from Hal.

Using his willpower, Hal also created a pair of giant green scissors. He used them to cut through the tough webbing. When they snipped through the last beam, he was free.

In the meantime, Kiriazis sent beams of yellow energy toward the green bird, slicing it in half. Just as it vanished, an oversized green flyswatter smacked her into the nearby yellow web. **THUD!**

"Caught in your own web?" joked Hal.

Kiriazis howled in anger. She netted a nearby asteroid and swung it toward Hal. He dodged it, but the large rock came at him again. Hal created a giant baseball bat. **THWACK!** He hit the boulder and sent it flying out of the asteroid belt.

"Home run!" Hal said, laughing.

Kiriazis flung herself toward him. She tackled Hal around the waist and they tumbled through the asteroid field. Hal grunted as they slammed into a space rock.

"Who's laughing now?" Kiriazis asked as she pinned him against the asteroid. He jerked his head to one side as a long spine from her back jabbed at his face.

ZZRRRRTT! Kiriazis toppled back as Hal's ring blasted her with energy. She tumbled a few times before coming to a stop.

Hal flew forward and the two slowly circled each other. "I should let the Jurans and the Talescians deal with you," he said. "There's nothing like a common enemy to bring people together."

Kiriazis' four eyes flared as she laughed. "They will never work together," she said.

"We'll see about that," said Hal as he raised his ring. He created two giant pairs of scissors and sent them toward the trapped fleets.

"Yes, Hal Jordan," said the Juran admiral. "Free us so we can defeat the Yellow Lantern."

Hal smiled at Kiriazis. "Told you!"

"And *then* we'll destroy the Talescian scum who control her," the admiral added.

Hal stopped smiling as Kiriazis burst into laughter. "Now, do you see?" she asked. "These two races will never learn. It is their hatred and fear that will make them so easy to control now that they're mine!"

"Not yours," said a shrill voice. "*Mine!*"

Hal spun around to see a familiar and ugly face.

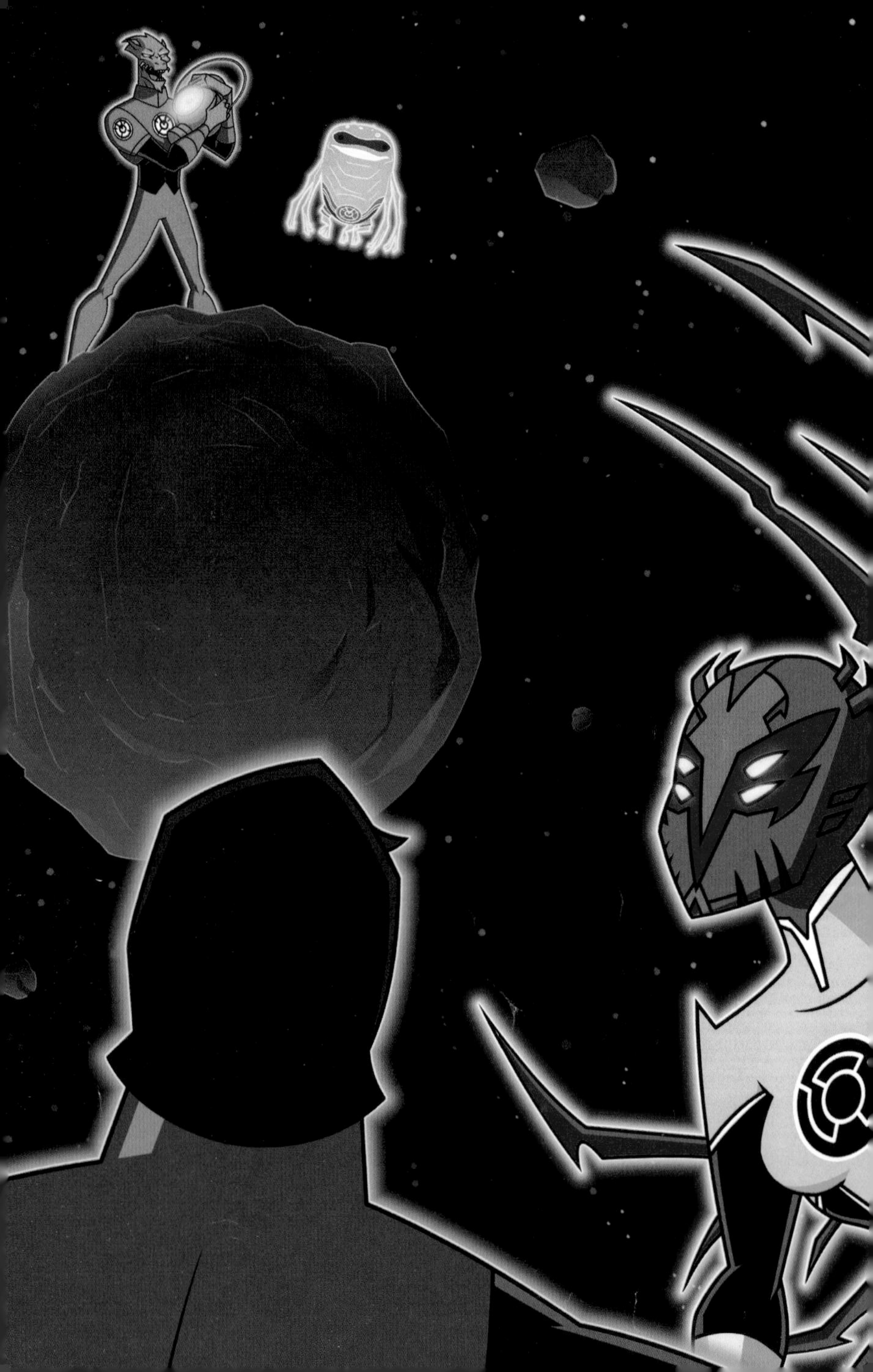

A tall alien was perched atop a large asteroid. His lips curled, exposing his many sharp tusks. He wore an orange and black uniform and clutched a large orange lantern to his chest.

He was Larfleeze, the one and only Orange Lantern.

Green Lanterns fought with willpower. Yellow Lanterns fought with fear. The Orange Lantern was powered by greed. Larfleeze was so greedy that he refused to let anyone else wear an orange power ring.

However, that didn't mean there was no Orange Lantern Corps. Just as Hal could use his ring to create green objects, the Orange Lantern used his ring to create his own troops. Every creature that was ever defeated by Larfleeze could be reconstructed as one of his Orange Lanterns.

Glomulus, the little Orange Lantern, crept up the asteroid and sat beside Larfleeze. He grinned up at Larfleeze and pointed toward the captured fleets.

Lafleeze nodded. "Yes, my pet," he said. "Once I have destroyed those ships, they will become a part of my corps."

Hal flew forward. "Not if I can help it, Larfleeze!"

The warthog-faced alien laughed. "And just how can you stop *me* and *my* entire Orange Lantern Corps?!"

Suddenly, the whole asteroid belt was littered with hundreds of orange creatures. Hal was surrounded by every size and shape of alien imaginable. They each wore an Orange Lantern Corps uniform. And all of them were charging at Hal!

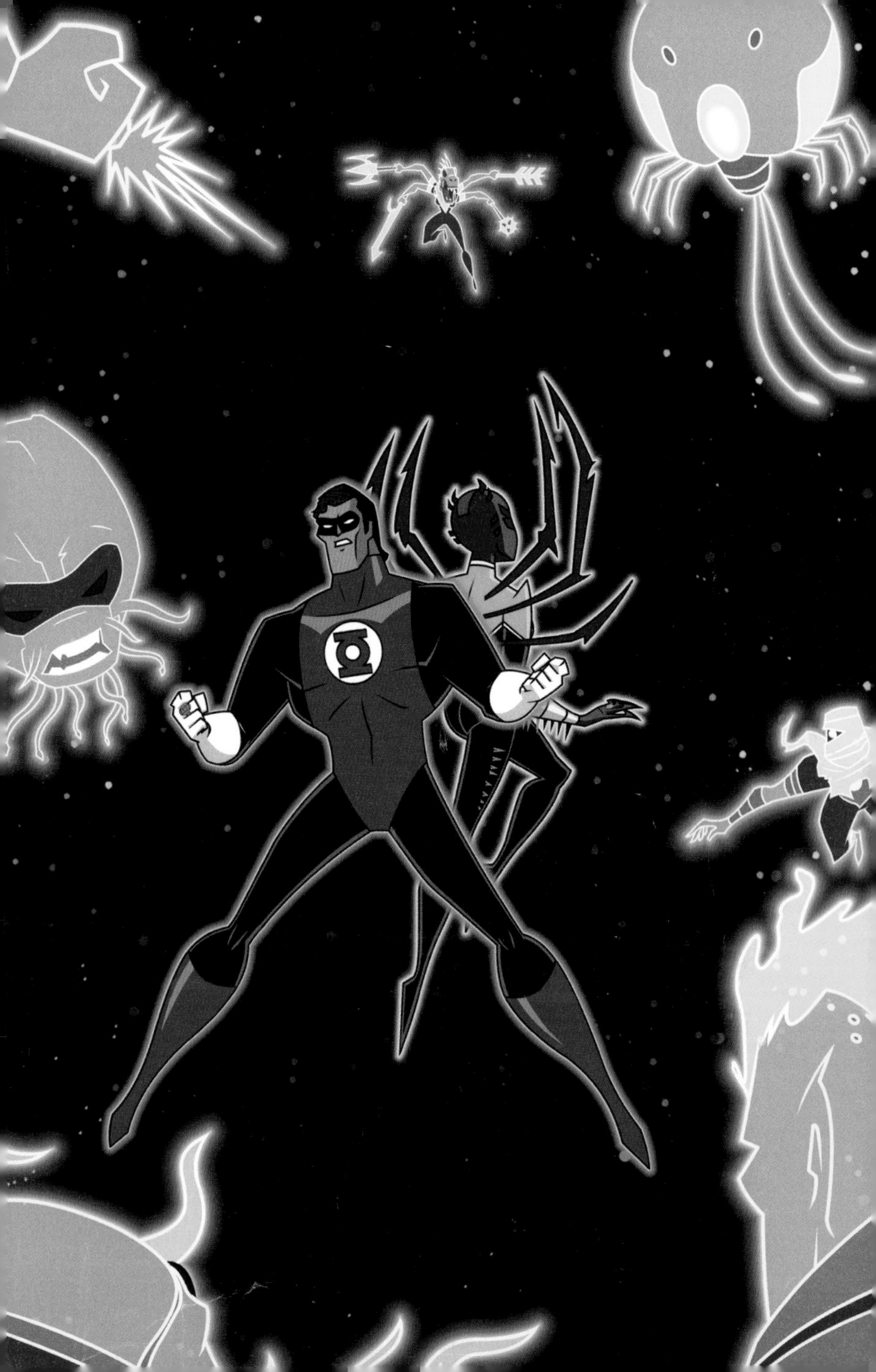

CHAPTER 4

LAST STAND

Hal Jordan and Kiriazis were completely outnumbered. Hal flew for his life. Orange Lanterns swarmed after him. He blasted a few away with green energy bursts. He ducked around asteroids as orange energy beams lashed out at him. He formed two large green shields to deflect the sharp claws from a crab-like alien. Hal knew that his ring wouldn't have enough power to hold them off for long.

Meanwhile, Kiriazis wasn't doing much better.

Orange Lanterns were overwhelming her, too. She managed to trap a few of them in her yellow webs. But she spent most of her time dodging and ducking attacks from others.

All the while, Larfleeze sat upon his asteroid. He kept the lantern clutched to his chest as he cackled at the show. "Yes, mine!" he bellowed. "They will be mine! Their rings will be mine!"

Hal swooped out of the way as a snake-like alien struck at him. SNAP! SNAP! Its two sharp fangs barely missed his head. Then Hal flew to Kiriazis and formed a green bubble around them both. Orange Lanterns blasted at the thin shield. He could barely keep the bubble from popping.

"Quick," Hal grunted. "Reinforce this shield with your ring."

Kiriazis faced him and sneered. It was clear from the look in her four eyes that she knew he was helpless. She spread her sharp claws and looked as if she were about to slice him to ribbons. But after a tense moment, she aimed her ring at the bubble and fired. **ZOOOM!**

Hal immediately felt relief as the power of her yellow ring added to his green. In fact, as the Orange Lanterns hammered the shield, he hardly felt a thing.

"It's clear that neither of us can defeat the Orange Lanterns alone," Hal said.

"Yessss," Kiriazis hissed.

"A temporary alliance, then?" she said.

"*Temporary*," Hal repeated. Kiriazis nodded in agreement.

Both of their rings glowed. **FLASH!**

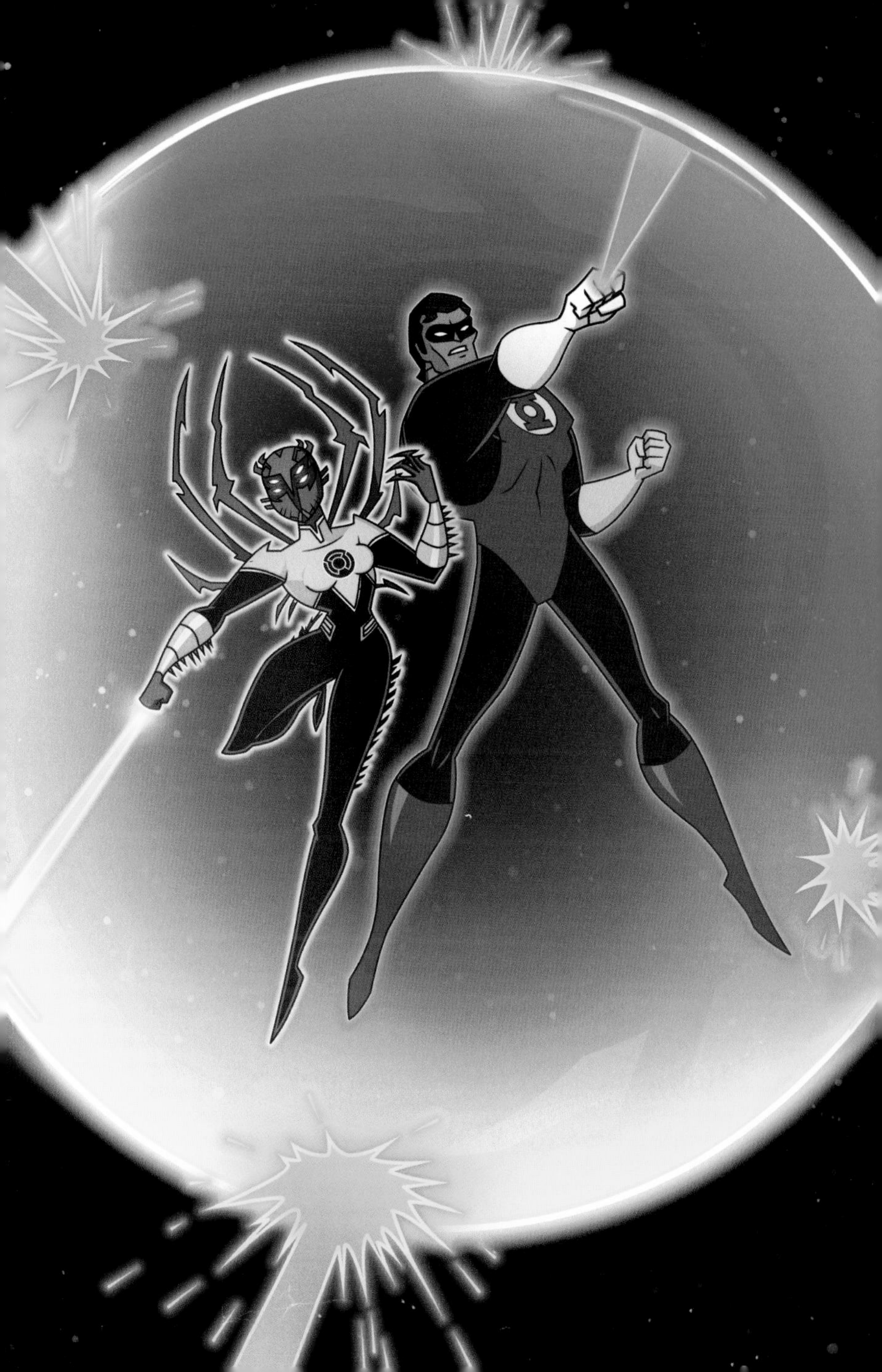

The shield exploded outward and Orange Lanterns flew everywhere!

"No!" shouted Larfleeze. "Get their rings! And then turn them into Orange Lanterns, too!" Beside him, Glomulus ducked into one of the asteroid's craters.

Hal and Kiriazis aimed together as they blasted Orange Lanterns. Beams of energy shot from their rings, intertwined, and then sent the attackers flying backward. They picked their enemies off one by one.

"There are too many of them," said Hal. "How about you make one of your webs?"

"With pleasure," said Kiriazis. She produced a large web from her ring.

Hal aimed his ring at the net. "Check this out," he said. Hal created what looked like a giant hoop with a long handle.

But when the hoop met the web, the yellow beams stretched out behind it. Together, they formed a green and yellow butterfly net!

Hal maneuvered the net so it scooped up as many orange attackers as possible. When the net was full, it fell away from the handle and kept all the Orange Lanterns trapped inside.

"No! No! No!" Larfleeze shouted. He turned to Glomulus. "Don't just sit there — go fight with the others!"

The little alien shivered then ducked back inside the crater. "Must I do everything myself?" Larfleeze growled.

The villain pushed off the asteroid and flew toward the group of netted Orange Lanterns.

Larfleeze held out his lantern and bathed the trapped aliens in orange light. They appeared energized as they flexed and pushed against the yellow webbing.

SNAP! Finally, the net broke open and they escaped.

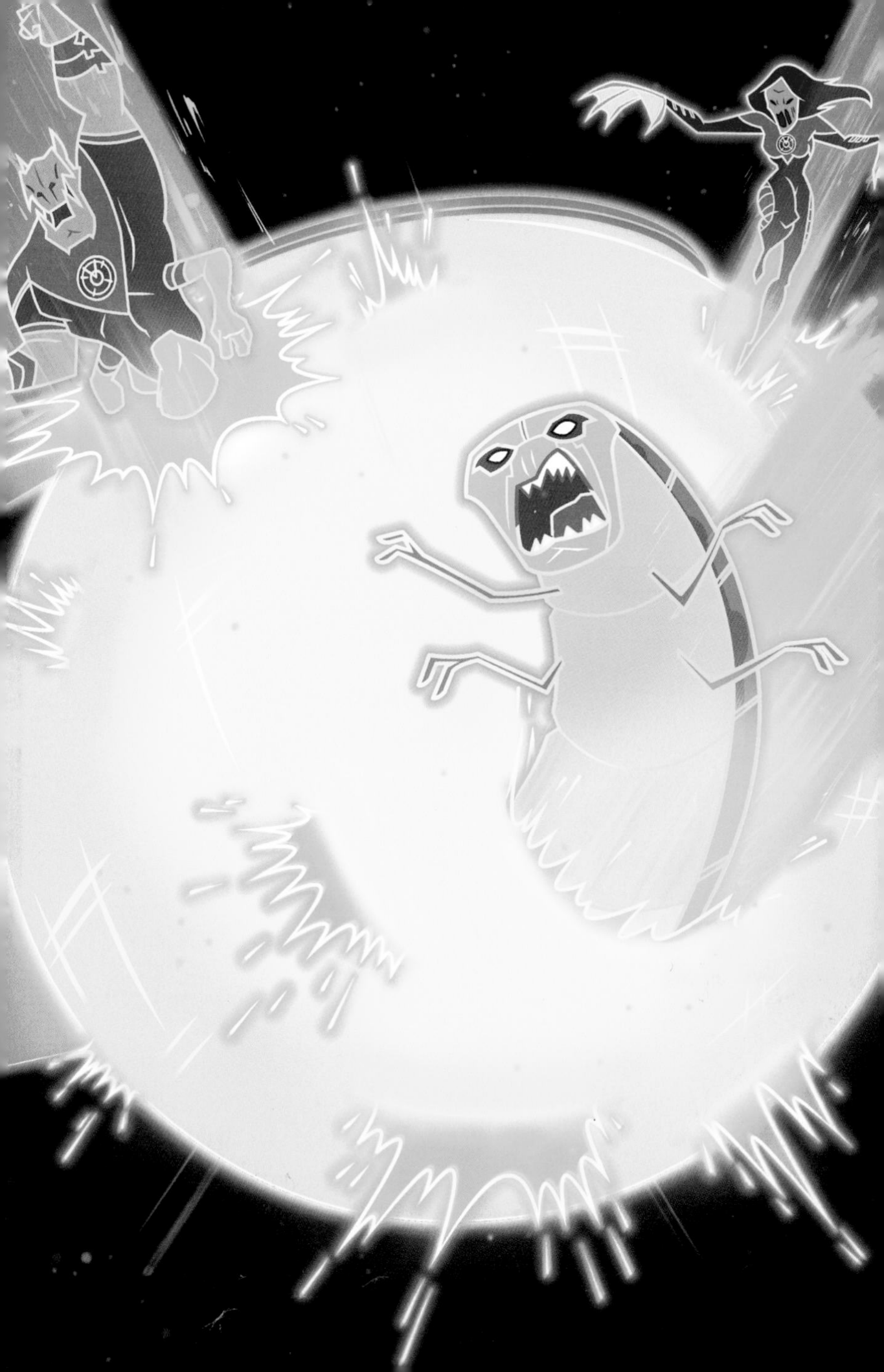

As the Orange Lanterns continued their attack, Hal turned to Kiriazis. "We have to stop Larfleeze himself."

"There is just one problem, Hal Jordan," said Kiriazis. She pointed to the warships behind them. "I cannot fight the Orange Lanterns and keep the ships trapped at the same time."

Hal's eyes went wide as the web surrounding the fleets vanished and the ships moved toward each other. Hal could hear their radio transmissions with his ring.

"Full speed ahead!" said the Juran fleet.

"Prepare to attack," said the voice of the Talescian commander.

The Jurans and Talescians were going to destroy each other, and there was nothing Hal Jordan could do about it.

CHAPTER 5

COMMON GROUND

Hal and Kiriazis continued to fight the Orange Lanterns as the fleets moved closer. Hal couldn't decide what to do. He didn't know if he could keep the fleets from fighting each other. And even if he could, the Orange Lanterns would quickly defeat Kiriazis and then come after the fleets anyway.

Hal turned back to the fight against the Orange Lanterns. Hal blasted two more of them. The least he could do was keep Larfleeze from winning.

He wouldn't let Larfleeze turn any of the fleets' crews into more Orange Lanterns. Hal scooped up another group of orange aliens, but Larfleeze freed them almost as fast as he could catch them.

PHWOOT! A beam of light shot past Hal and Kiriazis. It struck Larfleeze square in the chest. He tumbled backward.

Hal looked back to see both fleets flying side by side. They were in tight formation and began blasting the Orange Lanterns. The attacking aliens ignored Hal and Kiriazis and flew toward the warships. The ships' large guns continued to fire, keeping the aliens back. The Jurans and Talescians were working together!

"Now you and I just need to take care of Larfleeze," said Kiriazis.

"I was thinking about that," said Hal. "What's a good emotion to battle greed?"

Kiriazis smiled. Or at least Hal thought she was smiling. It was difficult to tell with her spider-like face. "Fear," she said. "Wanting everything is one thing. But imagine the fear of *losing* everything."

"Well, you *are* the expert on fear," admitted Hal.

Kiriazis narrowed her four eyes at Larfleeze. She raised her hand and aimed her ring. Soon, a yellow version of Larfleeze appeared. It flew toward the original.

"Give me the lantern," said the yellow Larfleeze. "It's mine!"

The real Larfleeze clutched his lantern tighter. "Nooooooo!" he howled. Kiriazis made another yellow Larfleeze appear.

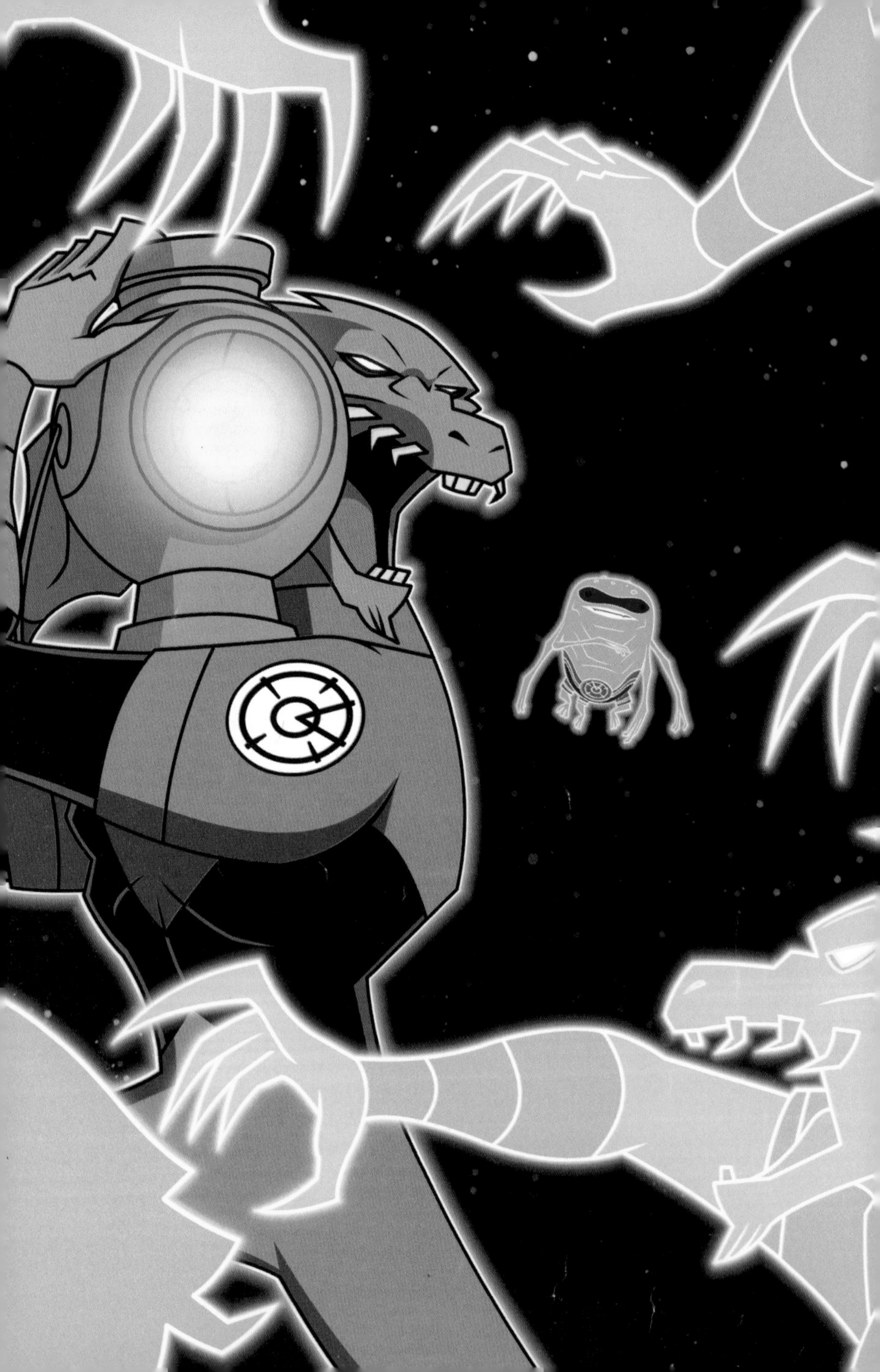

"No, it's mine!" the copy cried. And then another copy appeared. "Mine!" it yelled.

Soon, hundreds of yellow Larfleezes appeared. All of them chanted, "Mine! Mine! Mine!"

The real Larfleeze couldn't take it anymore. He flew away from the asteroid belt, yelling all the way. "No! You can't have it! IT'S MINE!"

When Glomulus saw his master leave, he scurried away in fear. The other Orange Lanterns vanished. The battle was won!

The two fleets held their positions as the delegates' ship moved closer. Hal raised his ring and contacted the ship. He saw both the Juran and the Talescian delegates through the main viewport. He heard their voices through his ring.

"It appears we owe you an apology, Lantern Jordan," said the Juran delegate.

"Yes," agreed the Talescian. "I actually agree with the Juran for once."

"Just doing my job," Hal said. He turned to Kiriazis. "Now, what about you?"

The Yellow Lantern tensed and her ring glowed. "Yes, what of me, Hal Jordan?"

Hal scratched his head. "Well, after all that talk of having a common enemy bringing people together," he sighed, "I guess it wouldn't set a good example if I fought you now, would it?"

Kiriazis' ring dimmed and she relaxed. "No, I don't think it would."

VROOOOM!! A purple energy beam shot from the delegate ship. It trapped Kiriazis inside a purple sphere.

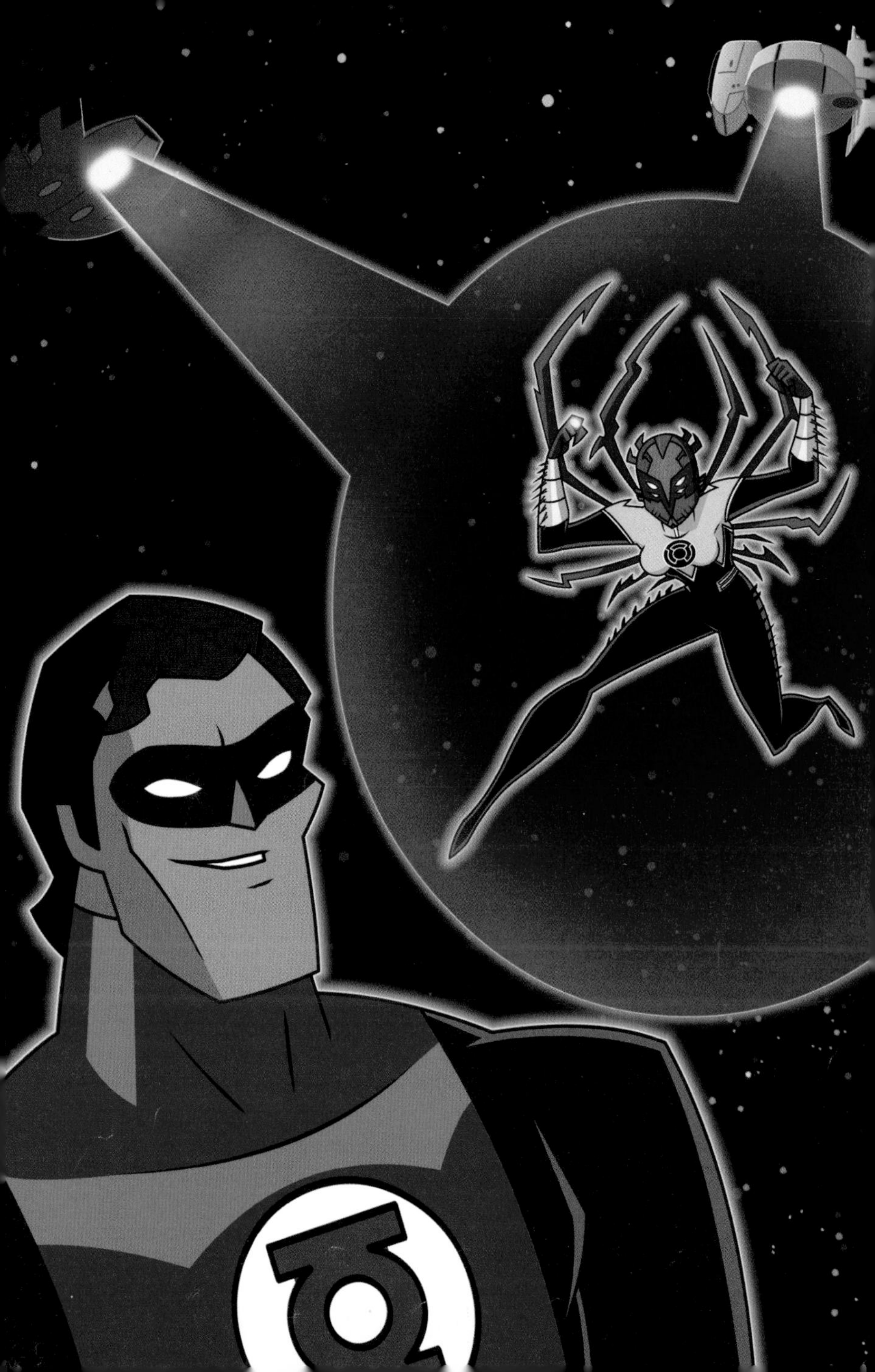

"We make no such promise," said the Juran delegate. "You must stand trial for your crimes."

"I agree again," said the Talescian. He gave a small chuckle. "Look, we just agreed again! This is getting easier by the minute."

Kiriazis pounded against the energy bubble. The Yellow Lantern growled. "They cannot do this!"

Hal shrugged. "Well, you did capture both their fleets and then threaten to conquer and enslave their people. I can see why they wouldn't want to let you go."

"You will pay for this, Jordan!" Kiriazis snarled. "No prison will hold me. You'll see!"

Hal ignored her threats and returned to the ship.

Once he was inside, the craft flew out of the asteroid field. Both fleets took up formation behind the smaller ship. Their guns were trained on the trailing force field holding Kiriazis.

It looked as if Hal would complete his mission after all. The Jurans and Talescians were well on their way toward lasting peace. Of course, Hal knew he couldn't take all the credit. He looked out the rear viewport at the angry Kiriazis. The Yellow Lantern beat, blasted, and pounded against the force field, but it held steady. She was the real reason the two worlds were coming together.

"A Yellow Lantern saved my mission," Hal said to himself. He let out a small chuckle. "This one's going to be hard to explain to the other Green Lanterns."

KIRIAZIS

REAL NAME: KIRIAZIS

OCCUPATION: YELLOW LANTERN

HEIGHT: Unknown

WEIGHT: Unknown

POWERS/ABILITIES: Ability to create power constructs with her ring; can also use her spider-like body to transform her ring's energy into a yellow webbing that can trap her foes and steal their energy.

BIOGRAPHY

Kiriazis is the Yellow Lantern of Sector 1771. As a member of the Sinestro Corps, Kiriazis has a gift for instilling fear in others. Before being recruited by Sinestro, Kiriazis reigned over a small planet in Sector 1771. While there, she destroyed all visitors to her realm, making her one of the most feared individuals in the entire galaxy. Her evil ways caught the attention of the Sinestro Corps, and she was made a Yellow Lantern. Ever since, she has been spreading fear, and deadly webbing, wherever she pleases.

Kiriazis was once trapped in a power ring crystal, but she eventually escaped from the energy prison.

Once, Kiriazis was captured by the Star Sapphires and reconditioned to spread love instead of fear. However, the transformation didn't last, and soon she returned to her terror-inducing lifestyle.

Kiriazis is entirely devoid of love and compassion. She has been known to use her power ring against even her family and friends.

BIOGRAPHIES

Michael Steele has been in the entertainment industry for almost twenty years. He worked in many capacities in film and television production from props and special effects all the way up to writing and directing. For the past fifteen years, Mr. Steele has written exclusively for family entertainment. For television and video, he wrote for shows including *WISHBONE*, *Barney & Friends*, and *Boz, The Green Bear Next Door*. He has authored over sixty books for various characters including Batman, Shrek, Spider-Man, Garfield, G.I. Joe, Speed Racer, Sly Cooper, and The Penguins of Madagascar.

Dan Schoening was born in Victoria, B.C., Canada. From an early age, Dan has had a passion for animation and comic books. Currently, Dan does freelance work in the animation and game industry and spends a lot of time with his lovely little daughter, Paige.

GLOSSARY

asteroid (ASS-tuh-roid)—small chunks of rock that travel through space. Asteroids are most common between Earth and Jupiter.

corps (KOR)—a group of people acting together or doing the same thing

deflected (di-FLEKT-id)—made something go in a different direction

delegate (DEL-uh-guht)—someone who represents other people during a meeting

fleet (FLEET)—a number of ships, planes, or other vehicles that form a group

negotiation (ni-goh-shee-AY-shuhn)—discussion between two groups where an agreement is sought

patrolled (puh-TROLLD)—traveled around an area to protect it or to keep intruders out

traitors (TRAY-turz)—people who betray their country or group, or people who are unfaithful or false to a friend or cause

DISCUSSION QUESTIONS

1. If you were Hal Jordan, would you have let Kiriazis go at the end of the story? Why or why not?

2. Hal's ring is fueled by willpower. If you had a power ring, what emotion or feeling would you use to fuel your powers? Discuss your answers.

3. This book has ten illustrations. Which one is your favorite? Why?

WRITING PROMPTS

1. Kiriazis feeds on the fear of others. What kinds of things scare you? Write about some times when you've been frightened.

2. Hal and Kiriazis work together to take down the Orange Lanterns. Have you ever worked with someone else to achieve a common goal? Write about it!

3. If you had Hal's power ring, what would you do with it? Would you fight crime and protect the universe? What would you fight for? Write about your life as a super hero.

MORE NEW

Green Lantern

ADVENTURES!

ESCAPE FROM THE ORANGE LANTERNS

ESCAPE FROM THE ORANGE LANTERNS

RED LANTERNS' REVENGE

RED LANTERNS' REVENGE

FEAR THE SHARK

FEAR THE SHARK

SAVAGE SANDS

SAVAGE SANDS

PRISONER OF THE RING

PRISONER OF THE RING

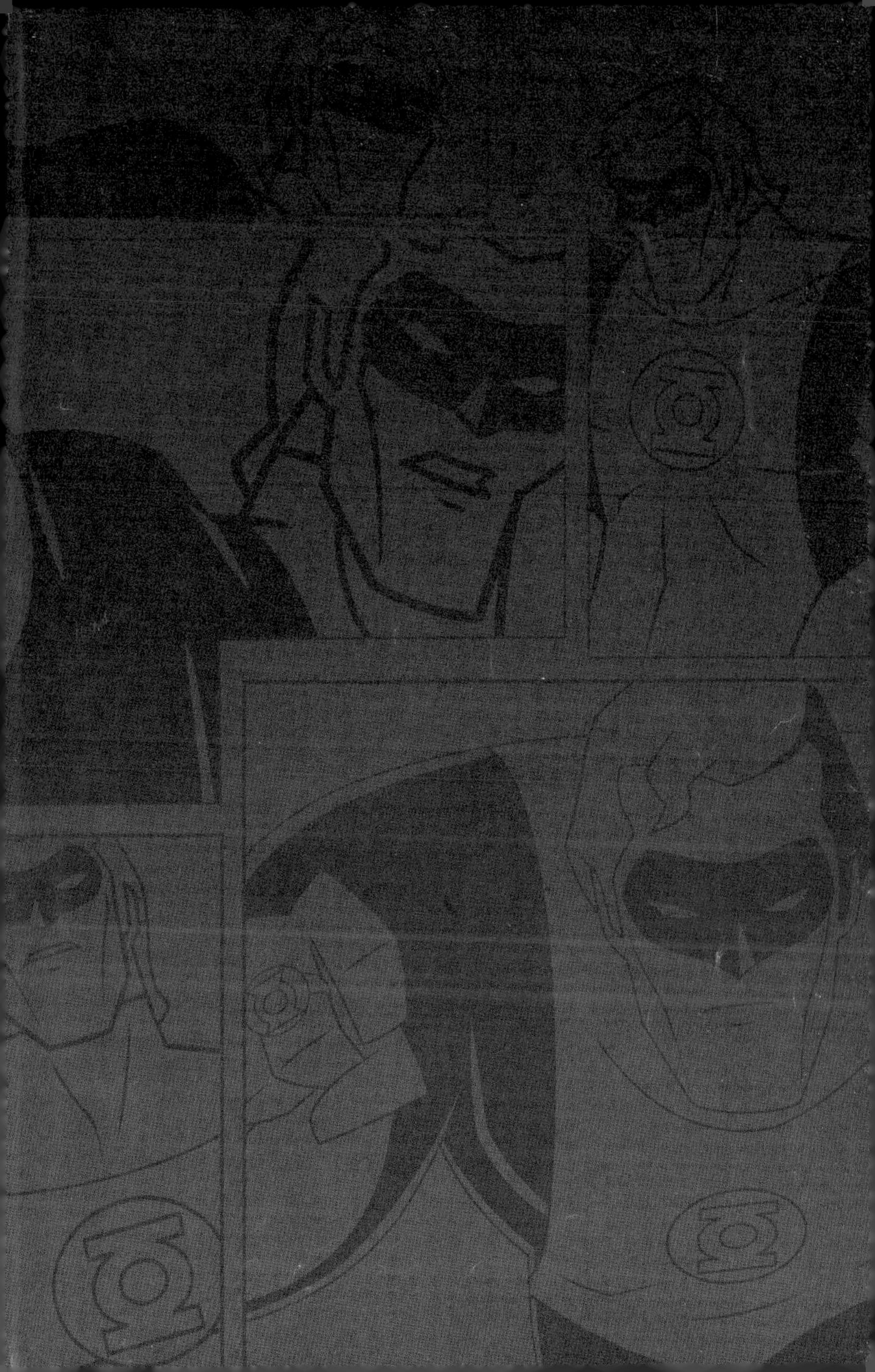

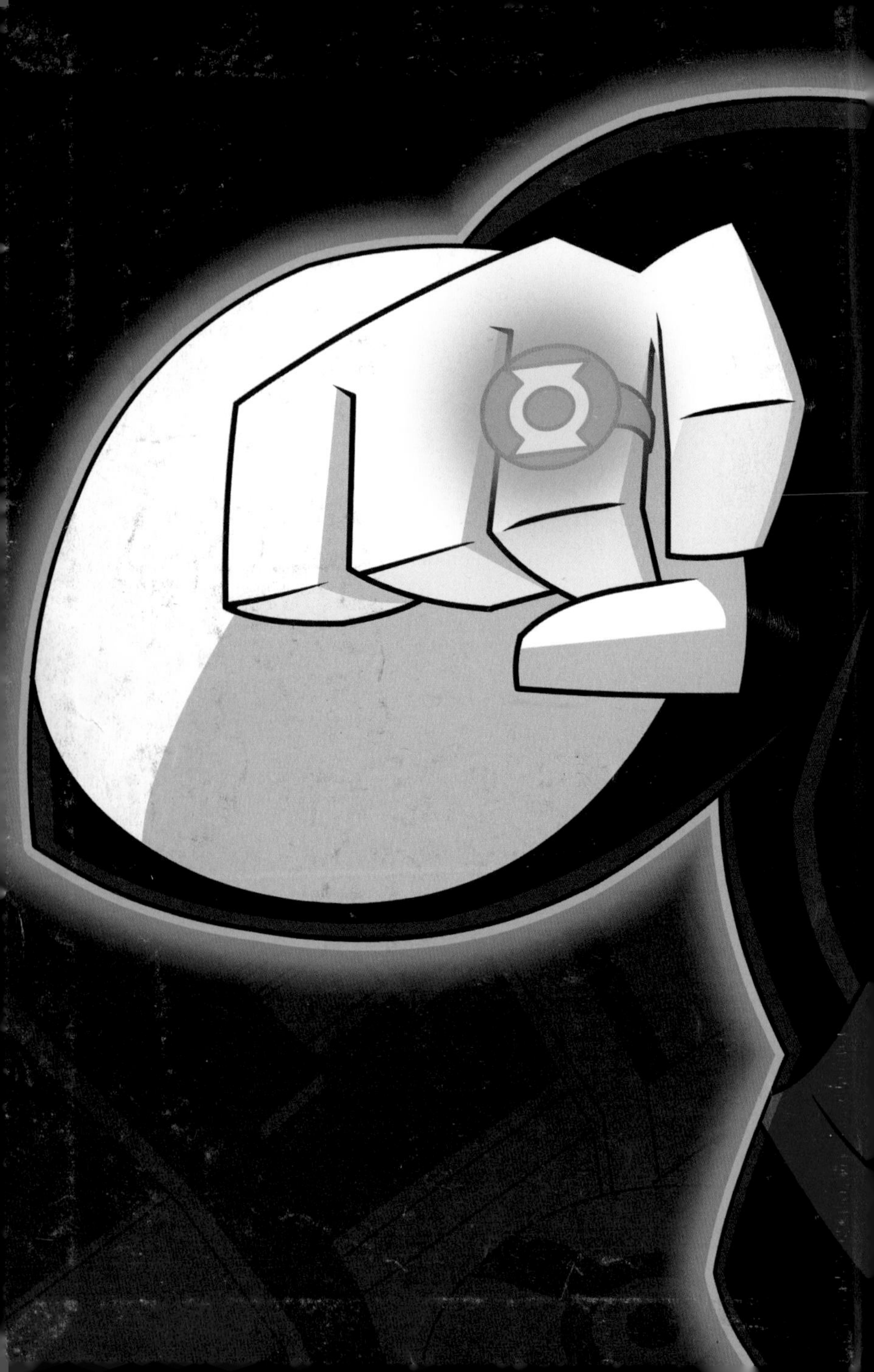